OLIVIA™

and the Fashion Show

adapted by Ellie Seiss
based on the screenplay "Olivia's Fashion Show" written by Silvia Olivas
illustrated by Patrick Spaziante

Based on the TV series *OLIVIA*™ as seen on Nickelodeon™

SIMON SPOTLIGHT

An imprint of Simon & Schuster Children's Publishing Division
New York   London   Toronto   Sydney
1230 Avenue of the Americas, New York, New York 10020
For information about special discounts for bulk purchases, please contact Simon & Schuster Special Sales
at 1-866-506-1949 or business@simonandschuster.com.
Manufactured in the United States of America 1013 CWM
8 10 9   ISBN 978-1-4424-2028-1

Olivia and her grandmother are going to a fashion show!
"I hope we see lots and lots of red clothes!" Olivia says.
"Me too!" says Grandma. "Fashion shows are always so exciting."

"I thought the clothes would be fancier," Olivia says to Grandma.

"Me too!" says Grandma. "A child could put on a better fashion show than this."

"A child like me?" Olivia asks.

"Certainly!" replies Grandma. "With your sense of style, Olivia, you could make beautiful clothes!"

That gives Olivia an idea. . . .

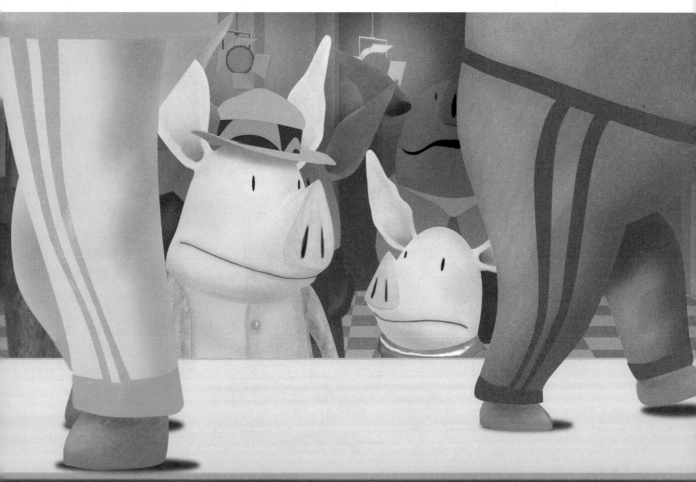

All of the judges agree—Olivia is a natural!

Olivia wants to design her very first outfit.

But first she needs supplies.

"Do you like my newspaper design?" Olivia asks.
"I think it's very fashionable and the hat is very . . . informative," says her father.
"It's stunning, Olivia!" exclaims her mother. "Do you think a glamorous designer could take her place at the dinner table?"

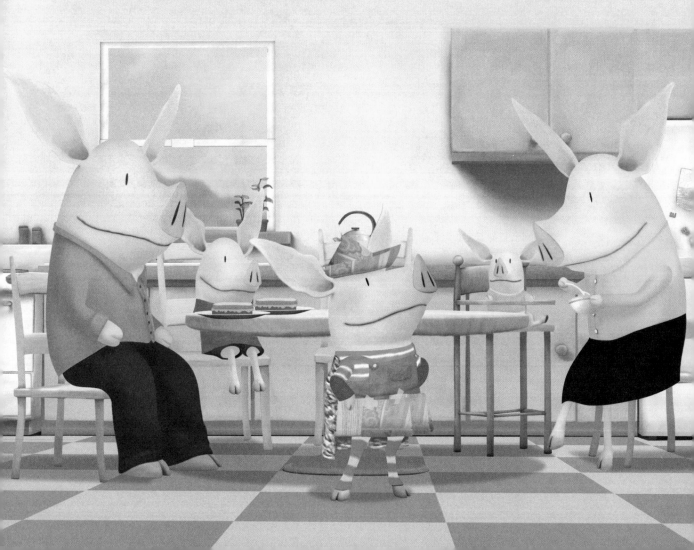

"Your attention, please!" Olivia declares. "I would like to announce the showing of my first fashion collection this Thursday at five forty-five sharp. All are welcome!"

Olivia asks Julian, Francine, and Ian to model her designs a the fashion show.
"But I don't want to be in your fashion show," says Julian.

"But I'm making an outfit just for you. It's what all
of the rock stars are wearing," says Olivia.
"They are?" Julian asks.
"They will when they see this," replies Olivia.

"Stop moving, Ian," says Olivia. "I'm trying to glue on your sleeves."
"But one more level and I'll be the ruler of the galaxy!" says Ian.
Olivia sighs. "How am I supposed to work like this?"

"Don't you just love it?" Olivia asks, holding up the dress she made
for Francine.

"No," replies Francine.

"Why not?" Olivia asks.

"Well, first of all, it's got *vegetables* on it," says Francine. "And it
needs ruffles." Olivia pulls lettuce-leaf ruffles out of her bag and adds
them to the dress.

"I could work with this," says Francine.

It's time for Olivia's fashion show!

"Where's the dress I made for you?" Olivia asks.

"Well, purple is my new favorite color," Francine explains,

"so I decided to wear this outfit instead."

Olivia makes a few last minute adjustments.

"Where's my guitar?" asks Julian. "I can't go out on the runway without my guitar! I can't look at the audience."

"Hmmm . . . what if you don't have to?" says Olivia.

Putting on a fashion show is hard work!

"Okay, Ian," says Olivia. "You can wear your space helmet, or you can wear this invisible helmet I designed."

"Awesome!" says Ian.

"What a magnificent show!" says Grandma.

Use the stickers
to put outfits on
Olivia, Francine,
Julian, and Ian. If
you don't press too
hard, then you can
reuse the stickers.